SARDAR'S SECRET WAR: ADVENTURES OF AN INDIAN SPY

APPALLA YAZNA SURYA SAI KIRAN

Made with ♥ on the Notion Press Platform
www.notionpress.com

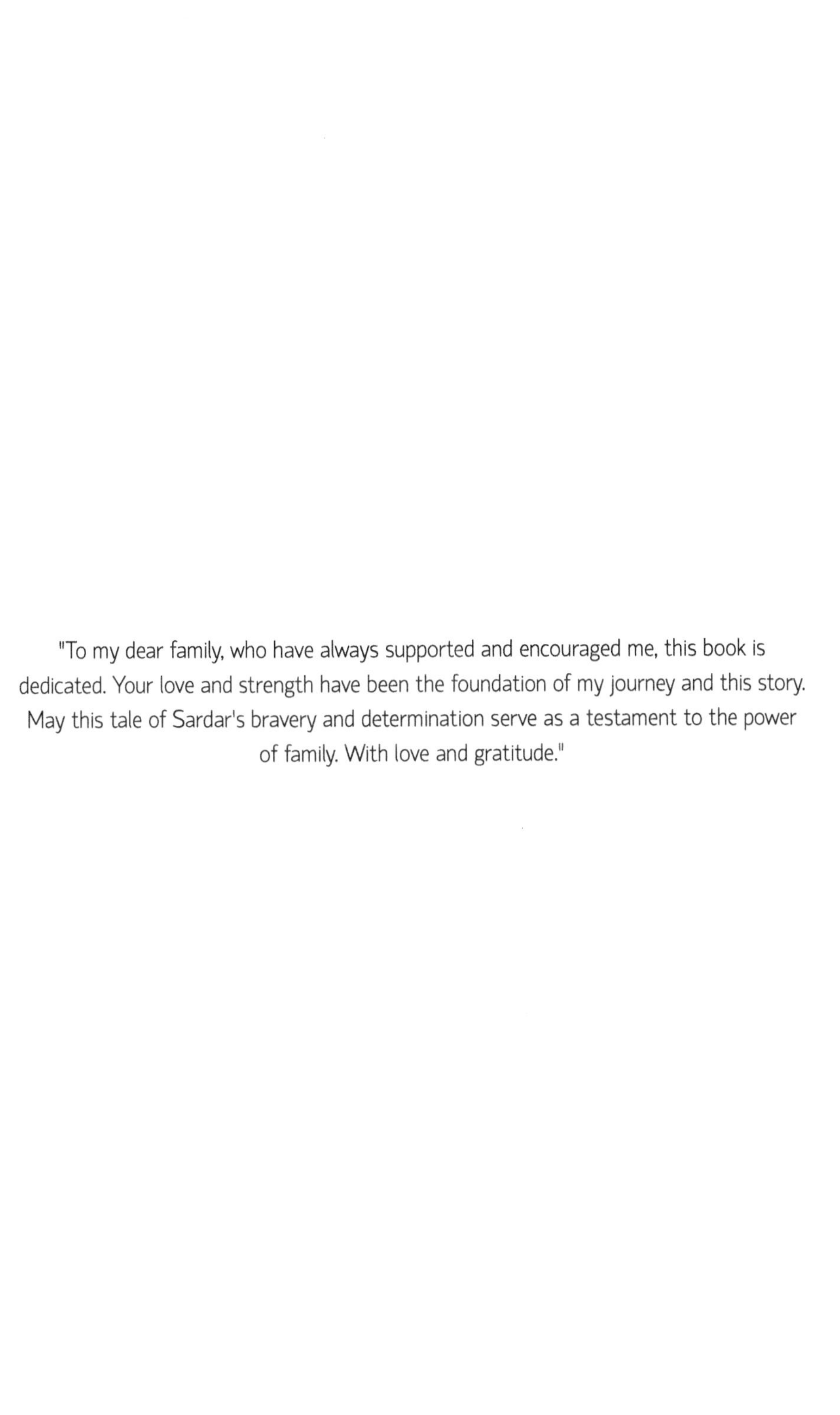

"To my dear family, who have always supported and encouraged me, this book is dedicated. Your love and strength have been the foundation of my journey and this story. May this tale of Sardar's bravery and determination serve as a testament to the power of family. With love and gratitude."

Contents

Foreword

In "Sardar's Secret War: Adventures of an Indian Spy," readers are taken on a thrilling journey through the life of Sardar, a fearless and cunning spy tasked with saving India from a dangerous and elusive threat. This page-turning novel is a testament to the bravery and determination of those who work tirelessly to keep our country safe. Join Sardar as he navigates treacherous terrain, outwits dangerous enemies, and faces the ultimate test in his quest to protect his homeland. Get ready for a wild ride filled with action, suspense, and intrigue.

Preface

"Sardar's Secret War: Adventures of an Indian Spy" is a thrilling journey of a daring spy tasked with saving India from the brink of destruction. Follow Sardar as he navigates through dangerous territories and takes on the toughest challenges in his quest to protect his country. Get ready to be captivated by the action, suspense, and drama of this page-turner.

Acknowledgements

First and foremost, I would like to express my heartfelt gratitude to all those who have made this book a reality. This book would not have been possible without their unwavering support and encouragement.

I would like to thank my family, friends and colleagues who believed in me and my story, providing me with the motivation to bring it to life.

Finally, I would like to thank the readers for taking the time to read this book. Your support means the world to me.

Prologue

The world of espionage is filled with mystery and danger, but for Sardar, it's a calling. As one of India's top spies, he's been tasked with stopping some of the country's greatest threats. From tracking down dangerous criminals to thwarting terrorists, Sardar's life is filled with excitement and adrenaline. But his latest mission will test his skills like never before. Join Sardar on his latest adventure, as he navigates the dangerous underworld of illegal arms trading, decodes encrypted messages, and battles to stop a nuclear disaster. "Sardar's Secret War: Adventures of an Indian Spy" is the story of a true hero, risking everything to protect his country.

About Me

I'm A.Y.S.Sai Kiran, a writer and huge fan of crime fiction and mysteries. Writing has been my passion since I was young, and I love crafting intricate characters in the world of law enforcement and detective work.

I was born and raised in Rampachodavaram, and my fascination with law enforcement and the bravery of those who protect the innocent has always inspired me.

I enjoy seeking out new and exciting stories when I'm not lost in writing. Being part of the crime fiction community makes me proud, and I can't wait to keep bringing exciting characters to life for readers everywhere. Thanks for joining me on this thrilling journey!

Previous Books

DETECTIVE GURUNADAM: THE CASE FILES
CBI Chronicles: The Cases of Officer Ranjit

SARDAR

Sardar is a skilled and cunning Indian spy, known for his quick thinking and ability to navigate complex situations. Born and raised in India, he was trained from a young age in the art of espionage and has since become one of the country's most valuable assets. Despite the danger and high stakes of his work, Sardar approaches each mission with a cool and calculated demeanor, never losing his focus or letting emotions cloud his judgment. Whether working alone or as part of a team, he always gets the job done, using his intelligence, charm, and combat training to outwit his enemies and keep his country safe.

Sardar is a daredevil in his work, never hesitating to take on even the most dangerous missions. With a keen sense of adventure and a thirst for excitement, he relishes the opportunity to put his skills to the test and push himself to the limit. Despite the risks involved, Sardar never backs down from a challenge, always confident in his ability to overcome any obstacle and emerge victorious. Whether he's jumping out of airplanes, infiltrating enemy territory, or facing off against heavily armed opponents, Sardar approaches each task with a fearless and determined spirit, never letting anything stand in his way.

Sardar has a sister who is an army commander and shares his daredevil spirit but is also known for her silly and playful personality. Despite her high-ranking position and serious responsibilities, she doesn't take herself too seriously, always finding time to joke around and have fun. However, when the situation calls for it, she transforms into a fierce and capable leader, respected by her troops and feared by her enemies. Her playful nature and sharp mind make her a valuable asset both on and off the battlefield, and she is always ready to lend a hand to her brother and support him in any way she can.

Sardar is a man of many talents. In addition to his spy skills, he is also a master of several languages, an expert in cryptography, and a talented marksman.

Despite his dangerous line of work, Sardar has a great sense of humor and often uses it to diffuse tense situations. He is known for his quick wit and ability to make even the grimmest of situations a little more bearable.

Growing up, Sardar was fascinated by the stories of legendary spies and often dreamed of one day becoming one himself. His desire to serve his country and make a difference in the world drove him to pursue a career in espionage.

While Sardar is fiercely loyal to his country, he also has a strong sense of justice and will not hesitate to go against his superiors if he feels that they are acting unjustly. He is a man of principle and will always do what he believes is right, even if it means putting himself in harm's way.

Despite the high stakes and constant danger of his work, Sardar has a strong sense of adventure and loves the thrill of the unknown. He relishes the opportunity to travel the world and experience new cultures and is always on the lookout for his next big challenge.

Sardar Team

Sardar: The team leader, as described previously.

Nisha: A former Indian classical dancer turned spy, Nisha is a master of disguise and espionage, using her charm and beauty to gather information and get close to her targets.

Rohit: A former Indian special forces soldier, Rohit is the team's heavy, specializing in close-quarters combat and explosive ordnance.

Priya: A tech wizard from India, Priya provides the team with cutting-edge gadgets and intel, and is responsible for keeping them connected and in the loop during missions.

Vikram: A former Indian intelligence agent, Vikram is the team's eyes and ears, gathering intelligence and conducting surveillance to provide the team with a clear picture of the battlefield.

This diverse team brings a range of skills and perspectives to the table, making them a formidable force in the world of espionage. Whether they're working together to take down a common enemy or competing against each other to complete a mission, they always find a way to work as a cohesive unit, using their strengths to overcome any obstacle and achieve their objectives.

Sardar's team is a group of highly skilled and trained Indian spies, who are tasked with carrying out missions that are too dangerous for conventional military forces. The team is led by Sardar, who is known for his bravery, cunning, and leadership skills.

CHARACTERISTICS OF SARDAR'S TEAM

Diversity: The team is composed of members from diverse backgrounds, with each member bringing unique skills and experiences to the table. This allows the team to tackle a wide range of missions and adapt to changing circumstances.

Cohesion: Despite their diverse backgrounds, the team works together as a cohesive unit. They trust each other implicitly and are willing to make sacrifices for the good of the team.

Training: The team is highly trained in a range of skills, including combat, surveillance, and espionage. They undergo rigorous training to ensure they can carry out missions with the highest level of proficiency.

Technology: The team has access to the latest technology and equipment, which they use to carry out their missions. They are equipped with cutting-edge communication devices, weapons, and surveillance equipment, which gives them a tactical advantage in the field.

Loyalty: The team is fiercely loyal to Sardar and their country. They will stop at nothing to complete their mission and protect their nation.

Sardar's team is known for their bravery, their cunning, and their ability to get the job done, no matter what the odds. They are considered to be among the best spies in the world and are feared by their enemies.

"SHADOW" (Strategic Homeland Analysis and Defense Operations Wing)

The SHADOW headquarters is a highly secure facility located in the heart of India, serving as the central hub of the country's intelligence-gathering and espionage operations. Accessible only to a select few and fortified with state-of-the-art security systems, SHADOW is the epitome of stealth and sophistication.

At the heart of the headquarters is the command center, a massive, high-tech room filled with rows of workstations, banks of computers, and walls of screens. Here, intelligence is analyzed and mission plans are developed, with operatives working around the clock to keep the country safe.

Adjacent to the command center is a secure communications center, where top-secret information is transmitted and received. The facility is also home to a training area, where spies can hone their skills, and a research lab, where new technologies are developed and tested.

Despite its highly classified nature, the atmosphere at SHADOW is one of camaraderie and shared purpose, with spies from all over India working together to keep their country safe. Whether they're relaxing in the lounge, working out in the gym, or grabbing a bite to eat in the mess hall, there's a sense of community and belonging that pervades the entire facility.

For those who work at SHADOW, it is a place of pride and purpose, a symbol of their commitment to their country and their dedication to their mission. Whether they're in the field or at headquarters, they know they are part of something greater than themselves, and they carry that knowledge with them wherever they go.

Advanced Security Measures: The SHADOW headquarters is protected by multiple layers of security, including biometric scans, retina scans, and voice recognition systems. The perimeter is monitored by surveillance cameras, and the facility is surrounded by high-tech defense systems to deter intruders.

Cutting-Edge Technology: The SHADOW headquarters is equipped with the latest and greatest in spy technology, including advanced communication systems, cutting-edge research equipment, and high-tech training simulators. This allows the spies to stay ahead of the curve and maintain their edge in the field.

Classified Information: The SHADOW headquarters is home to a vast wealth of classified information, including intelligence reports, operational plans, and confidential communications. All of this information is strictly controlled and monitored to ensure its security and integrity.

Operational Support: The SHADOW headquarters is staffed by a team of experts in areas such as communications, logistics, and research, who work around the clock to support the organization's operations. This enables the spies to focus on their mission and be confident that they have the resources they need to succeed.

Tight-Knit Community: Despite the highly confidential nature of their work, the spies at SHADOW are a close-knit community, bonding over their shared experiences and commitment to their country. They work together as a team, relying on each other for support and encouragement as they carry out their dangerous missions.

Kalthiran

Location: Kalthiran is located on the opposite side of the globe from India, and shares borders with several other neighboring countries.

Political System: Kalthiran is a politically unstable country, with a history of coups and civil wars. Despite this, it has managed to maintain a strong central government and is ruled by a powerful dictator who rules with an iron fist.

Economy: Kalthiran's economy is heavily reliant on its abundant natural resources, including minerals, oil, and natural gas. This wealth has allowed the government to maintain a large military, and to develop advanced military technology.

Military Strength: Kalthiran has a large and well-equipped military, with advanced weaponry, a powerful navy, and a capable air force. The country also has a well-established intelligence agency and is known for its aggressive foreign policy and military adventures.

Relationship with India: Kalthiran has a long-standing rivalry with India, and the two countries have a history of conflict and border disputes. The current government of Kalthiran is openly hostile to India and sees the country as a major obstacle to its ambitions. The two countries are engaged in a cold war, with each constantly seeking to gain an advantage over the other.

General Zafar Khalid

Name: General Zafar Khalid

Background: General Zafar Khalid rose to power through the military, and is a former commander of the Kalthiran army. He is known for his cunning and his willingness to use violence to maintain his grip on power.

Personality: General Khalid is ruthless, cunning, and highly intelligent. He is a master of propaganda and manipulation and has a charisma that allows him to inspire loyalty in those around him. He is known for his fiery speeches and his unpredictable nature, which keeps both his allies and enemies off balance.

Goals: General Khalid is driven by a desire for power and control. He sees himself as the only one capable of leading Kalthiran to greatness and is willing to do whatever it takes to achieve this goal. He is obsessed with crushing India and establishing Kalthiran as the dominant power in the region.

Methods: General Khalid uses a combination of brute force and cunning to maintain his grip on power. He is willing to use violence to eliminate his enemies and silence dissent and is not above-using propaganda and false flag operations to manipulate public opinion. Despite this, he has managed to maintain the support of key groups within Kalthiran, including the military, the intelligence agencies, and the business community.

Here's more information about General Zafar Khalid, the dictator of Kalthiran:

Early Life: General Khalid was born into a military family, and grew up in a disciplined environment. He showed a natural talent for leadership and strategy from an early age and was fast-tracked through the military academy. He quickly rose through the ranks and became known for his bravery and his willingness to take risks.

Rise to Power: General Khalid rose to power through a combination of luck, cunning, and brute force. He was involved in several successful military campaigns and became a hero to the Kalthiran people. He used this popularity to gain the support of the military and staged a successful coup against the previous government. He has since ruled Kalthiran with an iron fist, using his military might to crush dissent and maintain control.

Relations with Other Countries: General Khalid is a ruthless dictator, and is widely feared and hated by other world leaders. Despite this, he has managed to forge alliances with several other countries, including some of India's enemies. He is known for his unpredictable behavior and is not above changing alliances or breaking treaties to further his goals.

Personal Life: General Khalid is a private man, and little is known about his personal life. He is known to have several wives and several children. He is also rumored to have a secret network of spies and assassins, which he uses to maintain control and eliminate his enemies.

Legacy: General Khalid's legacy is one of fear and oppression. Despite this, he is revered by many Kalthirans as a strong and decisive leader, who has brought stability and prosperity to the country. He is widely seen as a symbol of Kalthiran's power and strength and is likely to be remembered as one of the country's most influential figures.

CHAPTER ONE

Saving India from Nuclear Doom: The Sardar Story

The rogue militants planned to launch a nuclear attack on India as a means of sending a message and striking fear into the hearts of the Indian people. They believed that the attack would give them leverage and help them to advance their own goals and objectives.

The militants had acquired a nuclear warhead and were planning to launch it from a remote mountain base in a neighboring country. They believed that this would allow them to carry out the attack without being traced back to their own country, and give them the best chance of success.

The intelligence about the nuclear attack was gathered through a combination of methods, including:

Electronic Surveillance: The Indian intelligence agencies monitored the communication of the rogue militants and their associates, intercepting emails, phone calls, and other forms of communication to gather information about their plans.

Human Intelligence: Indian spies and agents were planted within the network of the rogue militants, gathering information from the inside and reporting back to the intelligence agencies.

Satellite Imagery: The Indian government used satellites to gather images of the mountain base where the militants were planning to launch the attack, allowing them to map out the location and plan a mission to stop the attack.

Informants: The Indian intelligence agencies worked with informants who had information about the attack, offering them incentives and protection in exchange for their cooperation.

This information was combined and analyzed to give a complete picture of the attack and the plans of the rogue militants.

The Indian government assigned the case of stopping the nuclear attack to Sardar and his team because they were one of the best spy units in the country. They had a track record of success, and their skills and expertise made them the perfect choice for the mission.

Sardar and his team were known for their bravery and ability to carry out missions under pressure. They had extensive training in the latest spy technology, weapons, and tactics, and were well-equipped to handle any situation.

The Indian government trusted Sardar and his team to carry out the mission with the utmost professionalism, and they were confident that they would be able to stop the nuclear attack and save countless lives.

Sardar accepted the mission and immediately sprang into action, gathering his team and planning a strategy to stop the attack.

Sardar and his team gathered in their secret headquarters to discuss their plan to stop the nuclear attack. They carefully reviewed all of the intelligence they had gathered and brainstormed different strategies for disarming the warhead and stopping the attack.

Some of the ideas they discussed included:

Infiltration: Sardar and his team would sneak into the mountain base and disarm the warhead from the inside. They would use their training in stealth and spy tactics to avoid detection and carry out their mission.

Aerial Strike: The team would use military aircraft to launch a missile strike on the mountain base, destroying the warhead and the militants. This option carried some risk, as the missile could trigger a nuclear explosion if it hit the warhead.

Ground Assault: Sardar and his team would lead a ground assault on the mountain base, using their military training and weapons to fight their way in and disarm the warhead.

They weighed the pros and cons of each option, considering factors such as time, resources, and the safety of their team and the surrounding area. In the end, they agreed on a plan that they believed would give them the best chance of success.

With their plan in place, Sardar and his team sprang into action, putting all of their training and skills to use as they worked to stop the nuclear attack.

During their discussion, Sardar and his team also discussed the potential consequences of their mission. They considered the impact on regional stability, the relationship between India and the rogue militants, and the possibility of a larger conflict if their mission failed.

To minimize the risk to both themselves and civilians, they made contingency plans for various scenarios, such as the militants trying to move the warhead to a different location, or a change in the political climate that could impact their mission.

They also discussed the importance of keeping the mission confidential, as they were aware that any leaks could compromise the success of their mission. They made a vow to keep their mission secret and to complete it successfully, regardless of the obstacles they may face.

After their discussion, Sardar and his team felt confident and ready for the mission. They were determined to stop the nuclear attack and save countless lives, and they were committed to working together to accomplish their goal.

During their discussion, Sardar and his team also discussed the individuals involved in the attack. They believed that rogue militants had infiltrated the country and were working with a few corrupt Indians to carry out the nuclear attack.

They carefully analyzed the intelligence they had gathered, trying to identify the key players in the attack and their motivations. They realized that some of the corrupt Indians were motivated by money, while others were motivated by a desire for power and control.

Sardar and his team knew that they would have to be extra careful when dealing with the corrupt Indians, as they posed a significant threat to the mission. They would have to use all of their spy skills to outmaneuver them and stop the attack.

The team also discussed the possibility of a mole within their organization. They knew that they had to be on guard against the possibility of a traitor, and they agreed to be extra vigilant and to take additional security measures to protect themselves and their mission.

With their plan in place and their focus sharpened, Sardar and his team set out to stop the nuclear attack and bring the perpetrators to justice. They were determined to succeed, no matter what challenges lay ahead.

Sardar and his team identified several individuals who were aiding the rogue militants in their plan to carry out a nuclear attack. These individuals were corrupt and were willing to sell out their country for money and power. The following is a list of the individuals that Sardar and his team identified:

Rajiv Mehta: A wealthy businessman who was using his company to finance the militants' plan.

Sanya Patel: An influential politician who was providing the militants with inside information about India's security measures.

Kamal Singh: A high-ranking military officer who was providing the militants with access to military resources and weapons.

Arjun Sharma: A scientist who was using his expertise to develop the nuclear warhead for the militants.

Avi Gupta: A former intelligence agent who had turned rogue and was now working for the militants.

Nimesh Shah: An arms dealer who was supplying the militants with weapons and ammunition.

Sardar and his team were able to uncover several key clues during their investigation into the corrupt Indians involved in the nuclear attack. Some of these clues included:

Suspicious financial transactions: The team was able to trace large sums of money that were being transferred between the corrupt Indians and the rogue militants. This helped them to link the individuals involved and to understand their motivations.

Insider information: Sardar and his team were able to gather valuable information from their sources within the government and military. These sources provided them with valuable insight into the individuals involved in the attack and their movements.

Surveillance footage: The team was able to obtain surveillance footage from various locations, including the government agency that had been infiltrated. This footage provided them with visual evidence of the individuals involved and their activities.

Interceptions of communications: Sardar and his team were able to intercept communications between the rogue militants and the corrupt Indians. These communications provided valuable information about the plans for the nuclear attack and the individuals involved.

Analysis of social media activity: The team monitored the social media activity of the individuals involved in the attack. They were able to identify key individuals and gather additional information about their motivations and activities.

Arjun Sharma was an individual the team interrogated in their investigation of the nuclear attack. Despite the team's best efforts, however, Arjun remained tight-lipped and refused to reveal any information.

Sardar and his team tried various tactics to get Arjun to talk, including a good cop-bad cop, psychological pressure, and even physical intimidation. However, none of these methods seemed to work, and Arjun remained steadfast in his refusal to talk.

Frustrated by their lack of progress, the team began to suspect that Arjun was not just an ordinary member of the rogue militants, but perhaps a key player in the organization. They decided to escalate their efforts and intensify the interrogation, but still, Arjun remained silent.

In the end, the team was unable to get Arjun to reveal any information about the attack, and he remains a mystery to this day. Despite this setback, Sardar and his team continued their investigation, determined to uncover the truth and prevent the nuclear attack from happening.

Avi Gupta was another individual that Sardar and his team interrogated in their investigation of the nuclear attack. Just like Arjun Sharma, Avi proved to be a difficult nut to crack and refused to reveal any information about the attack.

Sardar and his team tried various methods to get Avi to talk, including psychological pressure, incentives, and even threats. However, Avi remained steadfast in his refusal to cooperate, and the team was unable to get any information out of him.

Despite their best efforts, Avi's silence only added to the team's suspicions that he was a key player in the rogue militants' plan. The team continued their investigation, hoping to uncover more clues and gather evidence that could help them get to the bottom of the attack.

During the investigation, Sardar and his team interrogated Nimesh Shah, only to discover that he was not an Indian citizen after all, but rather a Kalthiran citizen in disguise.

The team was shocked to find that Nimesh had infiltrated their country and was involved in the planned nuclear attack. They quickly realized that the threat was far greater than they had initially thought and that Kalthira was more closely involved in the attack than they had suspected.

When Sardar and his team interrogated Rajiv Mehta, they discovered that he had been forced to participate in the attack against his will. Rajiv's family had been taken hostage by the Kalthiran government, and he had been given no choice but to cooperate.

Sardar and his team listened carefully as Rajiv recounted the details of the attack and explained how he had become embroiled in the dangerous plot. They were shocked and saddened to hear of the lengths that the

Kalthiran government was willing to go to achieve its goals.

Rajiv Mehta was forced to participate in the nuclear attack against India by the Kalthiran government. They had taken his family hostage and threatened to harm them if he did not cooperate. Rajiv was left with no choice but to do as he was told, and he found himself caught up in the dangerous plot.

The Kalthiran government used a variety of tactics to keep Rajiv in line, including physical threats, psychological manipulation, and financial incentives. They constantly monitored his every move and kept him under tight surveillance to make sure that he followed through with their plan.

Despite the overwhelming odds against him, Rajiv held out hope that he would be able to find a way out of the situation and save his family. He struggled with feelings of guilt and shame, but he knew that he had to be strong for his loved ones.

During the interrogation, Sanya Patel revealed that Kalthiran had secret relationships with some countries. However, Sardar and his team already had some information about these relationships. Sanya provided more insights, but Sardar already had a good idea of the situation. The team continued to gather information and piece together the puzzle to find out the truth about the rogue militants and their plan for a nuclear attack.

During the interrogation, Kamala Singh revealed that the nuclear attack was going to happen within a month. This information was critical, and Sardar and his team quickly went into action to stop the attack. Kamala provided more details about the individuals involved, but her information was limited as she was also being forced to participate in the attack.

In the end, the team discovered that the attack was planned to take place at a large government facility in the capital city and that it was set to occur in just one month. They knew that time was running out, and that they needed to act fast if they were going to stop the attack.

Kamala reveals that "Black Tiger" is the mastermind behind the nuclear attack plan and the one giving orders to the rogue militants. Sardar and his team realize the urgency of the situation and intensify their investigation to locate and stop "Black Tiger" before it's too late.

Sardar and his team were getting close to finding the identity of the Black Tiger. Priya, who was the tech expert of the team, worked day and night to find any leads. After a week of hard work, she finally stumbled upon some valuable information on the dark web. A huge amount of money was transferred to a bank account with the initials "BT". Priya suspected that these initials could belong to the elusive Black Tiger. The team was ecstatic as they now had a new lead to work with. The bank account could hold key information that could lead them to the Black Tiger's real identity. Sardar and his team continued to work around the clock to get to the bottom of this mystery. The team decided to focus on the bank account named BT, with the hope that it might lead them to the identity of the mysterious Black Tiger.

Team Sardar was stunned when they received a parcel containing a confidential letter detailing the planned attack. The contents of the letter were alarming and they knew they needed to act quickly to stop it. The team gathered around, studying the letter in detail and discussing their next steps. The urgency of the situation was palpable and the weight of responsibility weighed heavily on their shoulders. They knew that time was running out and that they needed to work fast to prevent the attack from happening.

The letter that arrived was a game-changer for the Sardar team. It had confidential information about the planned nuclear attack and shocked the entire team. Half of the Sardar team started investigating the source of the letter. They were trying to find out who gave them the letter and how they knew about the attack. The team was on a mission to uncover the truth and find out all the details that were hidden in the shadows.

The team was able to track down the woman who delivered the letter by reviewing the CCTV footage. Using facial recognition software, they discovered that she was an undercover journalist who was working for the Indian government. This information made the team question the authenticity of the letter, and the investigation took a new direction.

Team Sardar interrogated the undercover journalist, named Aisha Khan, regarding the confidential letter and her connection to the Indian government. They asked her a series of questions, trying to get to the bottom of why she had given them the confidential letter and how she had acquired such sensitive information. The journalist remained tight-lipped, refusing to divulge any information that could compromise her mission or her sources. During the questioning, she revealed that while she was doing her undercover operation, she had heard the name "Black Tiger" mentioned multiple times. However, she stated that she did not have any further information about who this person was. She also added that the name was being mentioned heavily in New Delhi. This new piece of information added a new dimension to the investigation and the team was now focused on finding the mysterious figure known as the Black Tiger in New Delhi.

Sardar and his team were surprised to hear this information from Aisha Khan. They immediately realized that they need to go to New Delhi and search for this mysterious person named "Black Tiger". They knew that time was running out and they had to act fast to prevent the attack from happening. They thanked Aisha for the information and quickly left to start their next mission in New Delhi.

Sardar team quickly traveled to New Delhi after receiving the information from journalist Aisha Khan. Upon arriving, they discovered an illegal drug trafficking operation that was connected to the mysterious figure known as Black Tiger. Despite their efforts, the team was unable to locate Black Tiger or determine what he looked like. However, they were determined to continue their investigation and save their country from the impending attack. They were relentless in their pursuit, working tirelessly to gather any information that could lead them to Black Tiger and prevent the attack.

Determined to catch the mastermind behind the attack, Sardar's team decided to focus on the drug mafia. They believed that if they could catch everyone involved in the drug mafia, Black Tiger would eventually be caught as well.

To achieve this, they meticulously checked the bank statements and surveillance footage of the entire city. After hours of investigation, they finally got a lead. The lead pointed towards Nimesh Shah, whom they had arrested previously.

The team immediately went to question Nimesh Shah, hoping to get more information about Black Tiger. However, Nimesh Shah was uncooperative and refused to reveal any information.

Despite this setback, the team didn't give up. They continued their investigation and looked for other ways to gather information about Black Tiger. They talked to local informants and checked any other possible leads.

Days passed, and the team was no closer to finding Black Tiger. However, they didn't lose hope. They knew that the attack was imminent and they needed to find Black Tiger before it was too late.

The Sardar's team came up with a plan to catch the elusive Black Tiger who was behind the planned attack on the Indian borders. They decided to use Nimesh Shah, whom they had arrested previously, as bait. Nimesh was a key member of the illegal drug mafia that was believed to be connected to the Black Tiger.

The team put Nimesh in a room and placed a TV in front of him. On the TV, Nimesh saw a video of the successful attack on the Indian borders, and the attackers were seen marching toward India to take it down. As Nimesh watched the video, he felt happy. In his excitement, he accidentally revealed that the Black Tiger was not a man, but a woman.

This revelation was a breakthrough for the Sardar team. They had been searching for the Black Tiger for weeks, and now they finally had a clue as to their identity. The team immediately started to investigate the possibility of a female Black Tiger. They went through all the surveillance footage, bank statements, and any other available information.

After hours of intense investigation, the team found a lead. They found out that a woman had been making large transactions from different bank accounts. The transactions were made to fund the planned attack on the Indian borders. The team quickly realized that this woman was the Black Tiger.

Nimesh Shah revealed that he had heard that the Black Tiger had a big mole on her right thigh, which would help the team confirm her identity.

To confirm the identity of the Black Tiger, the Sardar team cross-checked the database of women and found two possibilities, one being Sardar's sister and the other, being Nazria Begum. Although Sardar's sister was investigated, she was found to be innocent. This left the team with only one option, to interrogate Nazria Begum.

The team was determined to find out the truth and save their country from the impending attack. They gathered all the information they could find on Nazria Begum and prepared for the interrogation.

Sardar team, determined to catch the elusive black tiger, was faced with a new challenge. Despite their extensive efforts, they were unable to gather any information related to Nazria Begum. The name itself was suspected to be a fake. However, Priya had an important update. She had found an invitation to an illegal party on the dark web and the user known as BT (whom they suspected to be the black tiger) was also attending the party. The problem was that the invitation was only for a male. Sardar, not one to shy away from a challenge, accepted the invitation and went to the party in disguise.

The illegal party was a high-stakes operation for Sardar and his team. It was their best chance to catch the black tiger, but it was also a dangerous situation. The party was filled with notorious criminals and Sardar had to be careful not to blow his cover. He mingled with the guests, trying to gather as much information as possible, and keeping an eye out for the mysterious BT.

As the night went on, Sardar learned that the black tiger was a highly sought-after figure in the criminal underworld. Many of the guests at the party were eager to meet the black tiger and offer their services. Sardar was getting closer to uncovering the identity of the black tiger, but he also had to be cautious. If he was discovered, he would be in danger.

After the encounter with the girl in a green dress, Sardar realized that she was the notorious criminal Nazria Begum. He knew that he had to act fast to gather information about her and her accomplices. So, he decided to use his seduction skills to get close to her and gather the information that he needed.

He approached her with a drink and started chatting with her, making small talk and gradually getting closer to her. As she drank the alcohol, she became more relaxed and open to his advances. Sardar then took her to a private room and started making out with her.

While they were in the heat of the moment, Sardar slightly tried to remove her pants and that's when he noticed a mole on her hip. He immediately realized that this was a crucial piece of information and he alerted his team via the communication system.

But Nazria quickly realized that Sardar was not whom he claimed to be and she quickly put on her clothes and ran away into the crowd. Sardar chased after her but she managed to escape.

Code red is an emergency protocol that Sardar activated when he found himself in a critical and dangerous situation, where his team was not close by to provide support. The protocol involves calling for backup from Bhavani, Sardar's sister who is part of the force.

As Sardar was surrounded by a group of armed criminals, he realized that he was in imminent danger and had no weapons to defend himself. In this dire situation, he made the call for help and activated the code red protocol.

Within minutes, Bhavani arrived on the scene with her team and launched an attack on the criminals, providing Sardar with a much-needed backup. The criminals were caught off guard and quickly overpowered.

Bhavani and Sardar then focused their attention on capturing Nazria, who was still trying to escape. However, Bhavani managed to catch her and deliver her to Sardar's team for further investigation and questioning.

Thanks to the code red protocol, Sardar was able to survive the dangerous situation and make significant progress in the investigation. The successful operation was a testament to the strength of Sardar's team and their unwavering commitment to protecting their country.

The interrogation of Nazria was a critical moment for the Sardar team. They had to get the information they needed to complete their mission and stop the planned attack on their country. The team used various tactics to extract information from Nazria, who was extremely resistant and unwilling to cooperate.

Despite the difficulty, the Sardar team was relentless in their efforts to get answers. They asked her a series of questions, trying to approach the situation from different angles. They also tried to build a rapport with her, hoping to earn her trust and get her to open up.

However, Nazria remained tight-lipped and didn't give away much information. The team tried to push her buttons and get her to react, but she was very composed and maintained her composure throughout the interrogation.

It was a tense and draining situation for the Sardar team. They were running out of time and needed to find a way to get the information they needed to stop the attack. They continued to ask questions, try new tactics, and push for answers, but it seemed like Nazria was going to keep her secrets locked away forever.

Despite the challenges, the Sardar team never gave up. They were determined to get to the bottom of the situation and protect their country, no matter what it took.

After interrogating Nazria, Sardar team went through her possessions and found an intriguing encrypted code. It was an opportunity for the team to gather new information and move closer to cracking the mystery behind the black tiger. The code was possibly the key to unlocking hidden information that could be crucial to their investigation. The team realized that cracking the code could be a challenge and they set to work immediately to decode it. They used various techniques and tools to decipher the code and finally, they succeeded in unlocking the encrypted message. The team was overjoyed with the discovery as the code led them to a new direction in their investigation. They now had a fresh lead to follow in their quest to apprehend the black tiger and end the illegal drug mafia in New Delhi.

The encrypted code read as follows:

dQWxq6UfTgJ0KzRvLsNi8ZpX9b1m3c7oHyP5h

This code appears to be a random combination of letters and numbers, with no immediately discernible pattern or meaning. It is likely that the code would need to be decrypted or hacked in order to uncover its contents, which could potentially hold valuable information or secrets.

After intense work decoding the encrypted code, the Sardar team finally got a new lead. This lead took them to the location of an underground illegal weapons supply ring. The team was taken aback by this new development, as they had never suspected the involvement of weapons in the drug mafia they were investigating. However, the team was relentless in their pursuit and was determined to uncover the truth and bring those involved to justice.

The location was a well-guarded facility, and the team knew that they would have to be cautious as they approached it. They devised a plan, utilizing all the resources at their disposal to gather information and prepare for their raid on the facility. The team worked through the night, making sure that all the details were ironed out and that everything was in place.

Finally, the day of the operation arrived. The team moved in, taking all necessary precautions to ensure that their mission was a success. They managed to get inside the facility and found a massive weapons cache, which was being guarded by a group of armed men. The team engaged in a firefight with the guards, exchanging bullets and taking cover as they advanced toward their objective.

Despite the odds stacked against them, the team emerged victorious. They managed to neutralize the guards and secure the weapons cache. The team then called in backup to take care of the rest of the operation, as they had uncovered a massive network that was involved in the illegal arms trade.

The team had finally succeeded in taking down a major player in the drug mafia and illegal weapons trade. The weapons cache was a significant find and provided a wealth of information that would aid in bringing the rest of the players to justice. The team was lauded for their bravery and commitment to their duty, and they were honored to have served their country in such a crucial operation.

The investigation was far from over, however. The team knew that there was still a long road ahead, and they were determined to see it through to the end. The discovery of the illegal weapons cache had given them new leads to follow, and the team was ready to tackle the next challenge that lay ahead.

The team was stunned to find such a sophisticated setup. The group was heavily guarded, with high-tech security systems in place to detect any intruders. The team approached the servers carefully, trying to avoid any alarms. After some time, they managed to find a way into the secure room where the servers were located. The servers were lined up in rows, with blinking lights and various gauges showing different metrics.

Sardar was shocked to see the sheer amount of power and technology at play here. The team quickly assessed the situation, taking note of the nuclear weapons control system, the satellite links, and the encrypted data stored on the servers. It was clear that this was a critical component of a larger operation, and the team needed to get as much information as possible and disable the systems as soon as possible.

Sardar and his team quickly sprang into action, trying to collect as much data as possible from the servers and making sure to cut any connections that might trigger the automated systems. Despite the intense pressure and danger of the situation, the team managed to work efficiently and effectively, collecting valuable data and disabling the weapons control systems. After a few hours of intense work, the team finally managed to secure the area, leaving behind only a few guards who were quickly overpowered.

The team then regrouped outside the facility, taking stock of the situation and debriefing each other on what they had discovered. They realized that they had uncovered a massive operation, one that was far more dangerous than they had ever imagined. It was clear that they would need to report back to their superiors immediately and plan their next move. But for now, they took a moment to bask in their hard-won victory, knowing that they had just made a significant impact in the fight against illegal arms dealers and nuclear proliferation.

Sardar and his team are now in a race against time. They know that they have a crucial mission ahead of them to locate the remote that controls the nuclear weapons. They start their search, going through every inch of the illegal weapons supply location, looking for any signs of the remote. They find a few leads, but they all turn out to be false.

Days are passing and the tension is growing. They know that they are running out of time. They cannot afford to waste a single moment as the fate of the nation is at stake. They keep searching and finally, after days of hard work, they find a hidden room with a lot of computer systems. One of the systems catches their eye. They examine it and find out that it is connected to the satellite network.

Sardar and his team immediately start trying to access the system. They face a lot of obstacles, including security firewalls and encrypted codes. But they are determined and their years of experience help them break through the barriers. They finally gain access to the satellite network and they find the remote that controls the nuclear weapons.

With the remote in their hands, they can now track the location of the nuclear bomb. They use all the information they have gathered to find the bomb.

As the deadline to disable the nuclear weapon was getting closer, Sardar's team was running out of options. Despite their efforts to extract information from Nazria, she still refused to speak. They knew that they had to resort to more extreme measures to obtain the information they needed.

Sardar and his team subjected Nazria to intense physical and mental torture. Day and night, they pushed her to the brink of her endurance. They did not give her a moment's rest, using all the means at their disposal to get her to open up.

The torture was brutal and unrelenting. They applied electric shocks, beat her mercilessly, and deprived her of sleep. Through it all, Nazria remained defiant, her lips sealed tight.

As the days passed, Sardar and his team began to lose hope. The deadline was fast approaching and they still had no leads on the location of the nuclear weapon. They were on the brink of despair when, finally, Nazria broke.

With a cry of pain, she revealed the location of the remote that controlled the nuclear weapon. She told them everything she knew, giving Sardar and his team the information they needed to find the remote and disable the bomb.

With this newfound knowledge, Sardar and his team set out on their mission to save India. The days ahead were going to be treacherous, but they were determined to succeed. They were prepared to do whatever it took to stop the weapon from being used.

Sardar and his team, along with the Indian military, arrived at the location they traced from the information obtained from Nazria. They were on high alert, as they knew that the situation was critical and that time was running out. As soon as they arrived, Sardar's keen eyes caught a glimpse of a man who was a most wanted criminal in India. The man was Judo, who had previously worked for a terrorist named Djinn.

Sardar didn't waste any time. He immediately launched an attack on the location, and his team and the Indian military followed suit. The attack quickly turned into a mini-war, with both sides exchanging fire. Sardar and his team were highly trained and well-equipped, but they were up against a group of ruthless criminals who were well-armed and determined to resist.

The fight was intense, with both sides suffering losses. Sardar and his team managed to push forward, making their way through the building and engaging in hand-to-hand combat with the criminals. They finally reached Judo, who was holed up in a secure room, surrounded by his henchmen.

Sardar and his team fought their way through the henchmen and finally confronted Judo. The two sides exchanged a few shots, and then Sardar managed to disarm Judo, bringing him down with a well-placed punch. Sardar's team secured Judo, and the Indian military secured the building.

With Judo in custody and the building secured, Sardar and his team started to go through the data servers they had discovered earlier. They found that the servers contained crucial information about the location of the nuclear weapon, as well as a remote control that could activate the weapon. Sardar and his team quickly realized the gravity of the situation, and they started working to disable the weapon.

They worked tirelessly, pouring over the data and trying to find a way to disable the weapon. They finally found a solution, and with the help of the Indian military, they managed to deactivate the weapon just in time. India was saved, and Sardar and his team had prevented a disaster.

Sardar and his team were hailed as heroes, and their names were remembered in the annals of Indian history. They had faced great danger, and they had triumphed in the face of adversity. They had saved their country and its people, and they had become legends in their own time.

Sardar will return.